DANGER
IN THE
JUNGLE TEMPLE

DANGER
IN THE
JUNGLE TEMPLE

AN UNOFFICIAL OVERWORLD HEROES ADVENTURE, BOOK THREE

DANICA DAVIDSON

Sky Pony Press
New York

Copyright © 2018 by Danica Davidson

Minecraft® is a registered trademark of Notch Development AB.

The Minecraft game is copyright © Mojang AB.

This book is not authorized or sponsored by Microsoft Corp., Mojang AB, Notch Development AB or Scholastic Inc., or any other person or entity owning or controlling rights in the Minecraft name, trademark, or copyrights.

All rights reserved. No part of this book may be reproduced in any manner without the express written consent of the publisher, except in the case of brief excerpts in critical reviews or articles. All inquiries should be addressed to Sky Pony Press, 307 West 36th Street, 11th Floor, New York, NY 10018.

Sky Pony Press books may be purchased in bulk at special discounts for sales promotion, corporate gifts, fund-raising, or educational purposes. Special editions can also be created to specifications. For details, contact the Special Sales Department, Sky Pony Press, 307 West 36th Street, 11th Floor, New York, NY 10018 or info@skyhorsepublishing.com.

Sky Pony® is a registered trademark of Skyhorse Publishing, Inc.®, a Delaware corporation.

Minecraft® is a registered trademark of Notch Development AB. The Minecraft game is copyright © Mojang AB.

Visit our website at www.skyponypress.com.

10 9 8 7 6 5 4 3 2 1

Library of Congress Cataloging-in-Publication Data is available on file.

Cover design by Brian Peterson
Cover photo by Lordwhitebear

Paperback ISBN: 978-1-5107-2704-5
Ebook ISBN: 978-1-5107-2710-6

Printed in Canada

DANGER
IN THE
JUNGLE TEMPLE

CHAPTER 1

"I'M WARNING YOU," THE VILLAGER TOLD US. "IF YOU enter that jungle temple, you'll never come out."

I felt my stomach clench. I was out with Dad, my cousin Alex, and my Earth friends, Maison, Destiny, and Yancy, on our way to a jungle temple that held a very special crystal shard. We'd recently learned that the evil Ender Dragon was trying to escape the End, and the only way we could stop her was to track down crystal shards left by my ancestor, Steve Alexander, before the monsters working for her could find them.

Steve Alexander had left a special book to help us find the shards, so that's how we knew one was supposed to be in the jungle temple. If we could find all the crystals, it would create the only weapon that could defeat the Ender Dragon. But even though the Ender Dragon was still in the End (for now), she had

Endermen and other mobs searching the Overworld for the same crystal shards. If she got her claws on the shards before we did, we'd not only lose our only chance to fight her, but it would make her more powerful than ever.

So far we'd managed to find two crystals, and finding and protecting them had been a serious challenge. Since I'd never been to the jungle biome before, I was especially unsure of what to expect. Seeing my nervousness, Dad had stopped in the village at the edge of the jungle biome to ask some questions.

"I didn't ask for a warning," Dad said to the villager in a gruff voice. "I asked if we were headed in the right direction."

Where I lived, everyone respected my dad because of his skills as a mob fighter and builder. But here, nobody knew him, and the villager was looking at Dad as if he were some kind of idiot.

"I can tell you're not from around here," the villager said. "That's why I'm trying to warn you."

"I've been to plenty of jungle temples," Dad said. He sounded insulted that anyone would doubt him.

"Doesn't matter," the villager said quickly. "There's jungle temples, and there's *that* jungle temple." He tilted his head in the direction we were going. "That one's haunted."

Maison, Destiny, and Yancy paled. Alex perked up. The more challenging the adventure, the happier

Alex was. I felt more like Maison, Destiny, and Yancy did.

"That's crazy," Dad said. "Temples aren't haunted."

"Something terrible happened in that temple, centuries ago," the villager said. "No one remembers exactly what, but we don't have to. Go anywhere close to that temple and it'll make your hair stand on end. Bad enchantments have cursed the place. Now they say armored ghosts prowl the halls like haunted guards. And if they find anyone skulking around, they take them directly to the dungeon."

"Dungeon?" Yancy mouthed at us. He'd been trapped in a dungeon once before, and I didn't think he wanted to return. He'd tried to stage a zombie take-over back in his days as a bully. But lately, Yancy was on the side of good.

"They say only one man has ever been able to escape from that dungeon," the villager went on, eyeing Dad. "If you want to risk it yourself, I can't stop you. But don't drag kids into it. One grownup and five children? Besides, these three kids look sickly."

He gave Maison, Destiny, and Yancy a once-over, clucking his tongue in sympathy and disgust. He didn't realize they were from Earth. "Those guards'll pick you off one at a time until no one is left."

"I've heard enough," Dad said, making a signal for us to follow him.

We did, though we couldn't help looking over our

shoulders, watching the villager as we got farther and farther away. He stood at the end of his village, shaking his head at us.

The village was quickly swallowed up behind us and we headed into the jungle proper. It was all so green, the trees lined with vines and the bushes covering the ground. Our passage was slow, because we had to climb on top of the vegetation or force our way through it.

"So, I'm going to go ahead and talk about the elephant in the room," Yancy said.

"Elephant?" I said, startled, looking around. "I think we just have ocelots and parrots here." I knew it was in a jungle biome that Dad had tamed an ocelot and turned her into our sweet cat, Ossie. Ossie was safe back at the house now, where my Aunt Alexandra was watching over the other crystal shards.

"It's a figure of speech," Yancy said. "We need to talk about the thing no one is talking about. See, I understand why we have to go to this temple to get the shard, but . . . what if that villager is right? Maybe we can just blow the whole temple up with TNT, and then look for the shard in the wreckage."

Dad looked at Yancy dangerously. I had a feeling Dad was still in a bad mood from his conversation with the villager, and he didn't want Yancy to remind him of it.

"TNT could destroy the crystal, and any other

clues we might find there," Dad said. "Besides, all jungle temples are more or less the same. They are all three stories tall. There are levers you can push to open a hidden trapdoor and get to a treasure chest. That chest is probably where the shard is, so we'll look there first. All that talk about 'armored ghosts' is pure nonsense."

I agreed with Dad on that one. I'd heard of and seen lots of crazy stuff, like talking Withers and portals to Earth. I'd even turned into an Enderman for a while, despite how dangerous it was (turning into an Enderman had let the Ender Dragon into my head, and she'd never fully left). She still liked to torment me in my mind, trying to get under my skin. But I'd never even heard of actual ghosts in the Overworld—especially armored ones!

"Wouldn't leaving the shard in the treasure chest be too obvious?" Yancy asked, but Dad silenced him with another look.

I'd been my dad's son for eleven years, so I knew the simple rule that Yancy didn't: don't question Dad, and things are a lot easier!

However, I was thinking the same as Yancy. Maybe normally the treasure was kept there, but if we could get the shard that easily, that meant the Ender Dragon's minions would be able to find it just as easily. Didn't it?

"What's that?" Maison asked, pointing ahead of us.

So far all we'd seen after leaving the village was jungle, jungle, jungle. Not a hint of humanity. But there was something white up ahead, and it was obvious next to all the green. It looked like . . . a sign?

The sign was partly covered by vines and leaves. Alex reached it first and wiped the green away with her hand.

Go no farther, the sign said. The haunted temple awaits.

CHAPTER 2

NDERNEATH THE WRITING WAS A DRAWING OF
several armored skeletons. But skeletons were
all over the Overworld, so that didn't seem like
a sign that the temple was haunted.

Then Maison said, "There's something on the
other side."

Alex walked around to the back of the sign.

"What does it say?" I demanded. Everyone was
crowded around so much that we were smooshing one
another and I couldn't see.

"It . . . doesn't say anything," Alex said. "It just has
a picture of a dragon."

The Ender Dragon! I was sure of it. But when I
pushed through to see it, I saw a picture of a dragon
with a little man riding on it. I was expecting an evil
looking dragon with claws and fangs and an appetite

for destruction. The armored skeletons on the other side looked way scarier than this dragon!

"The dragon picture looks much older than the skeleton picture," Dad said. "You can tell by how faded it is. It's like someone found an old sign and wrote their warning on the back." He shrugged and kept walking, even though the rest of us were still clustered around the sign.

"What do you think it means?" Maison said.

"I bet we find lots of clues at the temple," Alex said.

I tucked the sign into my toolkit so we'd have it for later. It might give us important information.

"Come on, kids," Dad called out. "I've timed this so we should reach the temple long before dark. We want to try to get in, out, and back to the village while we still have sunlight."

This was a good idea. Even though I was nervous about going to a possibly haunted temple, I felt safer journeying with my friends, especially with Dad and Alex. Maison, Destiny, and Yancy all played the game *Minecraft* and were good at it, and Alex and Dad had actually been to jungle biomes before and were great warriors. Alex was a master with her bow and arrows, and Dad had his diamond sword.

"Hey, look!" Yancy squealed. A navy blue parrot was flying overhead, beating its wings.

"Leave it, Yancy," I said. I was with Dad; we needed to stop dillydallying and get this done before dark. Alex gave Yancy a look that said the same thing.

"No, I want a pet parrot," Yancy said. "There's nothing like taming a bird to make you feel a little less . . . you know . . . *terrified* about going into a haunted temple. And I can teach it to say things and have it dance to jukebox music."

Then Yancy pulled something out of his backpack and began waving it around, going, "Here, Polly, Polly! Polly want a cookie? Polly want an Oreo?"

"Yancy," Destiny scolded lightly. She was his cousin and sometimes acted like the boss when Yancy was being weird. Which was often, because Yancy was Yancy. "Don't feed parrots cookies from our world."

"Why not?" Yancy said. "You can't feed parrots in our world chocolate, because it'll make them sick. That's why the programmers of *Minecraft* changed the game so you can only feed parrots seed, not cookies like you used to be able to. But now that I'm here in the real Overworld, I want to see what happens. Ah ha!"

Just then the navy blue parrot flew down to Yancy's eye level and took the Oreo, or whatever it was, eating it so fast that crumbs sprayed everywhere. Big hearts showed up around the parrot, showing that it loved Yancy now and it was tame. And it definitely didn't get sick, so it must not have been like parrots in Yancy's world.

"All right!" Yancy cheered as the bird perched on his left shoulder. He gave it another cookie, then wiped off the cookie crumbs that had fallen onto his shirt.

"Look, Destiny, I have a parrot on my shoulder. Don't I look like a pirate?"

"You look like an idiot," Alex muttered under her breath.

"Hey, parrot," Yancy said. "Can you say, 'Alex is a party pooper?'"

The parrot didn't try. He was trying to nudge his way into Yancy's backpack for more cookies.

"He is pretty cute," Destiny allowed after a moment. She reached out and stroked the bird's feathers. "You guys have some of the same types of parrots in *Minecraft* that we do on Earth. On Earth, this would be called a hyacinth macaw."

I hadn't known that, and I thought it was pretty interesting. I reached out to pet the bird.

"We'll call him Hyacinth, then," Yancy said.

"I'll never remember that," Alex complained.

"All right, we'll call him Blue," Yancy said, petting Blue on the head. "Nice and easy. Blue, we're looking for hidden treasure, just like the pirates of old stories."

I looked at Dad, wondering what he thought about all this bird business. But he wasn't really paying attention to us. Instead, he kept looking up, as if he expected something to jump down from the trees and attack us.

One thing that was nice about the jungle biome was that it didn't have special monsters in it. It had monsters—also called mobs—like zombies, creepers, and skeletons, but I could just as easily run into those at home. The only creatures that were specific to the jungle biome were parrots and ocelots, which didn't attack people.

I didn't think any of the bad mobs could get up into trees, but I looked up too. I didn't see anything scary. There were a lot of cocoa pods, though I wasn't going to tell Yancy that. Earlier he said he wanted to cut some cocoa pods in half and see if they made the sound of horse hooves like coconuts on Earth did. In the background, I heard Yancy trying to get Blue to say, "Argh, matey." Probably another Earth reference. Sometimes it felt like he never took anything seriously.

"This isn't right," I heard Dad whisper under his breath, as if he were talking to himself. Then he glanced back and saw me watching him. He shook his head and kept walking.

For a while we headed on through the jungle, with Dad striding ahead and the others cooing over Blue in the back. Yancy kept trying to get him to say things he thought were funny and Destiny told him were actually mean. Yancy replied that Blue had a sense of humor and knew where he was coming from.

I was half listening to all this, but mostly I was watching Dad's back. The way he was walking told me something was wrong, but he still wasn't saying what. Then he looked back up at the trees and said, "I knew it."

Everyone stopped.

"Is something in the trees, Uncle Steve?" Alex asked. We all looked up. Blue's head followed Yancy's gaze up too.

"No, not the trees," Dad said. "Look at the sky!"

It was hard at first, because so much of the sky was blocked by all the treetops. But I could see bits of a hazy, grayish sky. At first it didn't mean anything to me. Then I realized something.

The grayish color meant night was coming. It was darker in the jungle thanks to all the trees, so only Dad had realized that the light even above the treeline was off.

"That's not right!" Alex exclaimed. "We should have lots of time before dark!"

"Is this part of the temple being haunted?" Destiny asked, sounding scared. "Is this whole jungle haunted?"

We all looked at Dad. He was frowning angrily at the sky. I saw him clutch his diamond sword even tighter.

"Let's not take any chances," Dad finally said. "We'll run the rest of the way."

But it wasn't easy to run in the jungle. Trees and vines and thick bushes slowed us down. We soon found the most we could do was jog, and even that left us out of breath.

Now that Dad had pointed it out, I couldn't stop noticing that there wasn't enough light in the jungle. And the amount of light was rapidly dropping. I remembered something Steve Alexander had written in his book about the Ender Dragon: *As her power grew, she was able to change our very world. Night grew longer, giving her mobs more time to attack villagers and wreak havoc.*

So, in other words, the days got shorter?

Whether we were in a haunted jungle or the Ender Dragon was changing daylight hours, one thing was certain: as soon as it got dark, all the dangerous mobs would come out.

We weren't going to make it to the jungle temple and back before nightfall.

CHAPTER 3

PRETTY SOON, THE NIGHT WAS CLOSING AROUND us like a fist. We were still struggling through the foliage, our legs getting caught in vines. And there was no sign of the jungle temple!

"It can't be much farther," Dad was saying, hoisting himself over another bush.

"Shhh!" Maison said urgently.

We all froze. Even Dad froze, though he never took orders.

Maison was pointing.

We all followed the direction of her finger with our eyes, and our breaths hitched. Through all the trees, we noticed an Enderman shuffling through the jungle. It was far enough away that it hadn't noticed us yet. Normally Endermen were docile mobs that left us alone as long as we didn't look them directly in the eye.

But now that they were working for the Ender Dragon, they would attack us on the spot.

Endermen were really tall, and they had long arms and legs that swung wildy as they moved. With their tall, thin bodies and purple eyes, they were unique-looking, and they were also vicious when they turned against you. Their height helped them in fights, and so did their ability to teleport.

"Be as quiet as you can and follow me," Dad said in a low voice.

We tried, but it's not easy being quiet in the jungle. Our footsteps rustled through the bushes. Parrots were chirping in the trees and Blue was responding to them. Alex whispered harshly to Yancy, "Shush that bird!"

Blue, who still wouldn't say "Argh, matey!" or "Alex is a party pooper," or anything else Yancy was trying to get him to say, did not want to stop chirping. Yancy tried bribing him with cookies, but Blue would eat and then chirp again, and stopping for Yancy to get cookies out of his backpack was slowing us down.

"The Enderman won't care about a *bird*," Dad said. "Just keep moving."

"There's another one!" Maison said, pointing.

This Enderman was on the other side of us, just far enough away that we noticed it before it could notice us. It was digging through the bushes, as if looking for something. Little motes of purple light flashed up from its body, and they were bright in the incoming darkness.

I looked up at the sky. It was dark gray now, almost night. I thought I might have heard zombies in the distance. This was about the time they'd start spawning.

I made myself think about my ancestor, Steve Alexander, so I wouldn't get scared. Back in Steve Alexander's day, people in the Overworld didn't even leave their homes at night because there were so many monsters outside. These days we still had to be really careful, but Steve Alexander had made it so we could at least go out at night. He'd also found the Nether and the End and even Earth . . . the first person in the Overworld to ever do so. A trek through the jungle temple at night wouldn't be anything he couldn't handle, I was sure of it.

"There!" Maison said, pointing to a third Enderman. Thank goodness it hadn't seen us yet, either. We had to be getting close—and these Endermen were clearly looking for the crystal shard too.

I heard a growl from deep within the jungle, and it was definitely zombies. The light was fading so fast that it was getting hard to see, and Dad reached into his toolkit and pulled out a torch made of sticks and coal. Something ahead of us was even darker, so that it blotted out the sky and landscape. Was it a building?

We pushed aside more vines and all stopped to stare in horror and wonder.

We had uncovered the jungle temple.

CHAPTER 4

"THAT TEMPLE IS DEFINITELY HAUNTED," YANCY finally said. Blue let out a low whistle.

I looked at Dad, expecting him to tell Yancy there's no such thing as haunted buildings. But even Dad's eyes were wide, and he murmured, "I've never seen a temple like this before. This has to be ten times the size of any other jungle temple."

We all felt small next to the temple, lost in its shadow. It was made with mossy blocks, and even though it was three stories tall like other temples, it was so massive it looked like a sleeping monster. Like it would swallow us up and never let us out. I looked to the left and to the right, and the jungle temple kept going as far as I could see in both directions. Someone had spent a lot of time building this.

It also appeared abandoned, and so dark and lonely

that it was spooky. And for some reason it felt like something terrible had happened there. As if that terrible feeling had sunk into the walls like smoke.

"Follow me," Dad said. "These old temples tend to be full of trapdoors and booby traps. If you're not paying attention, you could trigger arrows that will fly straight for your face."

With only Dad's torch for light, we slowly crept up the old steps. I half expected the blocks to crumble under our feet, but they held. There was no door in the jungle temple, so the entrance simply yawned open, daring us to enter.

Once inside, we looked around cautiously. There was a long, dark hallway to the left and a long, dark hallway to the right. In front of us were steps that led down into more darkness. The mossy blocks that made up the temple made the air feel swampy and wet.

"Here," Dad said. He put his torch against the wall so it brightened the area around us, and pulled another torch out of his toolkit. Alex and I also pulled torches out of our toolkits.

Then Dad pointed down the steps. "This should lead us to the hidden room."

It felt like every step might trigger some kind of weapon. Dad tested each block with his foot before he let us follow him. The steps down to the basement went on and on until, finally, we reached a small room at the bottom. I was expecting two more long hall-ways, but this tiny room was obviously walled off from the rest of the temple basement. I wondered what was on the other side of those walls.

Dad led us to a set of three levers on the wall next to the stairs. "If you move the levers in the correct pattern, it will open a trapdoor leading to a hidden room on the floor above."

"Can't you just smash through the wall to the room behind it?" Alex asked eagerly. She looked ready to do some smashing.

"Technically, yes," Dad said.

"Stevie, can I borrow your swor—" Alex began. I knew she wanted my diamond sword because it was better than her arrows at breaking through walls.

"No," Dad said sharply. "That villager was exaggerating about a ghost, but he's right that this isn't like a normal jungle temple. Let's do everything the way we're supposed to, and we'll be less likely to trip any traps. Now . . ."

He studied the three levers. "In the past, every time I've seen levers on this side of a temple stairway they've all been set to the same pattern: right, left, left, right." As we watched, Dad moved the levers in that pattern. Nothing happened that I could see.

"Now we find the trapdoor," he said.

We slowly made our way back up the stairs. The trapdoor, Dad said, would be right next to the top of the stairs. However, when we got there, the floor looked the same as ever.

"Strange," Dad said, stroking his beard. "I want you kids to go back downstairs and try different patterns on the lever. I'll stay here and call to you if anything opens."

"Will you be okay on your own here?" Destiny asked.

"Yes, but you five stick together, no matter what," Dad said.

"Uncle Steve can handle anything," Alex told Destiny, who still looked a little worried. Then Alex said to Dad, "If the patterns don't work, can we smash—"

"Go," Dad said.

We went. Back down into the darkness on our own.

Alex tried different patterns on the levers, getting more and more impatient. After each pattern, we called up to Dad to ask if it worked. And after each pattern, he said no. I tried to do the math in my head about how many possible patterns we could try, and that made my brain hurt.

"This is stupid," Alex muttered after our seventeenth try. "Maybe the temple is so old that these levers are broken. What if they never work?"

That's when we heard Dad's bellow.

CHAPTER 5

"DAD!" I CRIED. WITHOUT EVEN THINKING ABOUT traps, I turned and ran up the steps as fast as I could. Dad wouldn't make a sound like that unless something was really bad! The Endermen might have snuck up on him!

Everyone else was running, too, right at my heels. But when we reached the top of the stairs, all we saw was . . . *nothing*.

The two hallways still stretched into the darkness. And the torch we had left on the wall was still there, crackling with fire. But Dad was *gone*.

"Maybe the trapdoor opened and he fell in," Alex said. "He must be trapped in that room!"

I didn't think Dad would be dumb enough to fall through a trapdoor he'd been expecting, but I didn't know what else it could be.

"Try that pattern again!" I told Alex. "We'll stay here and see!" Dad had said we shouldn't separate, but this was an emergency. If he had fallen through the floor and the trapdoor had closed back up by the time we got up here, it would probably open and close quickly the next time we did the pattern too—and we had to see what happened.

Alex dashed downstairs. A few moments later, I heard her shout, "Okay, I did it!"

Maison, Destiny, Yancy, Blue, and I stared at the floor, then at one another. No trapdoor had opened up.

"Are you sure it's the right pattern?" I asked. We'd done so many patterns they were starting to blur together in my head.

"Yes!" Alex called. "Let me try again. Okay, how about now?"

"No!" I called back, my heart pounding. What if the trapdoor would only open once? What if we couldn't get to Dad down there?

"Forget this, then!" Alex shouted. "I'm smashing through these levers!"

Despite what Dad had said, I was ready to try Alex's way. Anything to find him!

As we ran back downstairs, I could hear the smashing sounds as Alex took out the wall. Even arrows could break through walls if we needed them to.

"I got through!" Alex called. "But he's not here! There's just a chest in this room and—"

And then Alex let out a horrified scream.

CHAPTER 6

"ALEX!" I CRIED AS MY FEET HIT THE FLOOR AT the bottom of the stairs. The wall with the levers was destroyed, revealing a small room beyond it with a chest.

Dad wasn't there.

Alex wasn't there.

They had both disappeared without a trace.

"Wh-what happened?" I cried.

Maison put her hands on what was left of the wall and looked into the room. "Do you think . . . she fell through a trapdoor in there too?"

"It's haunted," Yancy said bluntly.

"No, it can't be haunted," Destiny said. "Steve must have fallen into this room, then fell through another trapdoor. Then Alex got in and fell through the same trapdoor. That has to be it."

"Then how come we heard Alex fall through the second trapdoor, but we only heard Steve make a noise once?" Yancy asked. "Shouldn't we have heard him fall through two trapdoors?"

"Well, the wall was busted when Alex fell," Destiny said. "So we could hear her better."

"That must be it," Maison said. "They're still in the temple and we've just gotten separated. But they're okay. They have to be."

I wasn't so sure. I'd never heard Alex scream before. Alex loved danger and risking her neck. She'd probably already fallen through her share of trapdoors while she was out exploring. It would take more than a haunted jungle to make her scream like that.

We'd done exactly what Dad had told us not to do: we had separated. And now Alex was gone. We'd lost our two best fighters in just a few minutes.

"It's okay, Stevie," Maison said, turning back to me and putting her hand on my shoulder. "They both still have their weapons. I'm sure they're fine."

I wanted to believe that, but I just couldn't. I remembered what the villager had said: *"If you enter that jungle temple, you'll never come out."*

"Dad!" I called as loudly as I could. "Alex! Where are you?"

The answer was silence. My heart was pounding like a piston.

"Let's get the chest," Maison said. "If it has the shard . . ."

She slowly crawled over the ledge and into the room, tapping each block with her foot until she got to the chest. She popped open the chest and . . .

All it held was paper.

Maison dug to the bottom, just in case the shard was hidden underneath. Nothing. I'd never heard of a treasure chest that kept paper in it, and I tried to see what the writing was. Most of the paper was so old it was crumbling, and the darkness in the temple didn't help. Then Maison lifted one of the papers toward our torchlight and I saw something that caught all of our attention.

It was a fancy S and A curled together: the symbol of Steve Alexander.

CHAPTER 7

STEVE ALEXANDER HAD ALWAYS LEFT THAT SYM-
bol near clues about the Ender Dragon or the
crystal shards!

"What does it say?" I cried.

Maison picked up the chest and returned to us on
the other side of the ledge. We all bent over it, holding
the torch just close enough to see the papers without
lighting them on fire.

Yancy picked up a sheet of paper and it fell apart in
his hands. "Hmm, this isn't working," he said.

"Yeah, but maybe these papers have a clue to where
the crystal shard is," Maison said. "Since it's not in the
chest."

"You also touched most of the floor in there,"
Yancy said. "And it didn't trigger any trapdoors."

"I didn't touch *all* of the floor," Maison pointed

out, still fishing through the papers and trying to find something we could read.

Yancy looked at Maison skeptically for a second, then reached into his backpack and pulled out a few items. He threw the items into the room, hitting all of the remaining blocks on the floor. Nothing happened. If weight was supposed to trigger them to open up, then being hit by objects should trigger them, too, I thought.

Slowly and without a word, Yancy crawled over the ledge and into the little room. He picked up the items he'd thrown, studying the ground around him. I knew he was investigating.

"Be careful," Destiny scolded lightly. "You don't want to trigger the trapdoor."

"There is no trapdoor," Yancy said. Just to prove his point, he started jumping on all the floor spaces, as though daring them to open up. None of them did. The bouncing annoyed Blue, though, and the little parrot flew off Yancy's shoulder and hovered in the air.

"Wait, I can read this!" Maison said excitedly, waving one of the papers. "It says, '*We cord . . . cord . . .*' I don't know how to pronounce this word."

Yancy stepped back over and read the paper. "'We cordially invite you to a feast in the jungle temple, where we celebrate the victories of Steve Alexander and J—'"

"J?" I said.

"Yeah, it just cuts off there," Yancy said. "Who's J? It looks like the start of a name."

Everyone was looking at me because I was the only one who had been in the Overworld their whole life. The truth was, though, I had no idea who J was! I only knew of Steve Alexander fighting battles on his own.

"Maybe his wife?" I guessed. "Or his son? No, wait, I think he named his son Steve . . ."

"Was there someone Steve Alexander teamed up with in his adventures?" Yancy asked. "Jeremy, Jordan, Jasmine? If I had Wi-Fi, I could Google a list of J names."

"There was Maya, but that doesn't start with a J," I said. Maya was the Earth woman Steve Alexander had found. She'd helped him hide all of the crystal shards.

"What does 'cordial' mean?" I asked. I'd heard the word before. Was it another clue?

"It just sounds like a typical invitation," Yancy said. "It means people are being invited in a kind way. But isn't that all invitations to parties? The real question is, who's J?"

Everyone was looking at me as if they expected me to know what to do next. With Dad and Alex gone, I was the only one left who had any real knowledge of the Overworld.

But I've never been in a jungle temple! I wanted to tell them. I thought back on everything Dad had taught me about jungle temples from his trips to them in the past, but this temple already seemed so different from the temples he'd told me about—it was bigger, and the levers worked different. Who knew what else would be odd in this place?

I looked at the S and A symbols and thought about Steve Alexander. During our last fight against the Endermen, I had thought I was hearing Steve Alexander's voice, giving me confidence. At the same time I had kept hearing the Ender Dragon's voice, and she had been mocking me and trying to bring me over to her side. She was still in the End, but she had ways of getting into my head.

I knew that, with as scary as this temple was, and with us all being alone now, it would be easy to give in to fear. I had to be strong like Steve Alexander. I had to.

"I think we need to search the whole temple," I said. "Even if it is haunted. For my dad and Alex, the crystal shard, and whatever else we can learn here."

I just hoped I was doing the right thing.

CHAPTER 8

WE WENT UP THE STAIRS. I TOOK ANOTHER look at where Dad should have been standing, just in case he had somehow reappeared. But the place where he had been standing was as empty as ever.

"The torch moved," Yancy said suddenly.

We all looked at where the torch hung on the wall. Dad had put it to the right of the entrance. Now it was on the left.

"Stevie's dad must have moved it," Destiny said.

"But . . . why?" Yancy said. "Why fuss with the torch when more important things are going on? I'm telling you, even if this place isn't haunted, one thing is obvious: we're not alone here."

Blue let out a low, spooky whistle. Everyone looked down the dark hallway, as if we expected to see someone—or something—creeping out of the blackness.

"Come on, let's look around so we can get out of here!" Destiny said, and started taking purposeful steps down one of the hallways.

"Destiny, no!" Maison cried, lunging forward. But she was too late—Destiny stepped on one of the blocks, and arrows shot out of the wall, heading straight toward her. Maison managed to grab her in time, knocking both of them to the floor. The arrows hit the other wall, quivering as they stuck in the blocks.

"Are you all right?" I said, hurrying over to them.

Destiny looked embarrassed and startled at the same time. Maison just looked relieved. Fortunately, neither of them were hurt.

"Slight change to Stevie's plan to look for clues," Yancy said. "Let's explore this place until we find Steve, Alex, and the crystal shard. Then let's get out of here. Whatever clues we find on the way, great. But I'm not staying here any longer than I have to."

"Fine," I said.

Blue settled back on Yancy's shoulder, but this time Yancy didn't crack any pirate jokes. We made our way much more carefully down the hallway, testing each step before taking it. This was going to be a long night.

A room opened up to our left and I moved the torch to shine into it. Then we all jumped back. The room was full of hulking shadows.

CHAPTER 9

I WAS SURE WE'D FOUND A ROOM FULL OF HOSTILE mobs, all ready to attack us. But when I looked more closely, I realized the hulking shadows were cast by old furniture—not anything that was alive.

We crept cautiously into the room. If the whole jungle temple felt haunted, this felt like the very center of the haunting, somehow. Like whatever awful thing had made this place haunted had happened right here. The furniture was all savagely broken, as if someone had gone a rampage, wanting not only to destroy, but to destroy completely. I saw what used to be tables and chairs torn to pieces.

In the torchlight, I also saw the wall was slashed with enormous claw marks.

"Here's another one of those invitations with Steve

Alexander's symbol on it," Yancy said, picking up a piece of paper. It was so old and eroded, it looked almost as thin as cobwebs.

"Does it say who J is?" I quickly asked.

"No," Yancy said, turning the paper over. "This one also cuts off, even before it gets to the J."

Maison put her hands to the claw marks on the wall. The marks were deep enough that she could fit her fingers into the grooves.

I continued to slowly walk into the room, testing the floor and holding the torch in front of me. There were chandeliers hanging from the ceiling, and they were so covered with cobwebs that they looked like white cotton candy from Earth. Our footsteps thudded loudly in the empty room.

I noticed some writing on the wall and stopped to check it out. Was it a message?

My heart jumped in my throat. The message read HELP.

The letters were shaky, as if whoever had written it had been trembling with fear as they did it. And there was nothing else—no more writing to tell me if they'd gotten the help they needed.

Yancy followed my gaze, saw the writing, and halted in his tracks. "Well, that's not creepy at all," he said sarcastically.

"Do you think someone is still trapped in this temple?" I asked. "I mean, people from before who tried to come in here?" If anyone was still stuck here, we had to find them and get them out!

"I doubt anyone would come here unless they had a really good reason," Destiny said.

"Maybe some treasure hunters who wanted a thrill," Yancy said. "A real Alex type."

As soon as he said that, I saw Yancy wanted to snatch the words back. He had reminded all of us that Alex was missing.

Could she have scratched this herself, trying to get our attention and tell us we were going in the right direction? No, it looked too old.

At the far end of the room was a giant raised area, like a stage. It was littered with more destroyed furniture, and I saw more claw marks on the stage floor and on the wall behind it.

I was so caught up in looking at the claw marks that I wasn't paying attention. I stepped on a floorboard and I heard something rattle. I jumped back, thinking arrows might fly out at me, the way they had with Destiny.

Then I saw the rattling was the sound of several door-sized holes in the walls opening up behind the stage and along the walls. Secret rooms! Maybe Dad and Alex were in one of these!

"Come on!" I called to the others, and we approached the closest door. My heart was jumping like a piston again. I stepped through, and was in for a shock.

CHAPTER 10

THE DOORWAY I HAD CHOSEN LED TO A GIANT room that circled the whole previous room. All those doors just led to this one area. Why would they need so many doors to one room? And why did it have to be hidden? Was there treasure here? I swept the torch over the wall, looking for any clues, like the S-A symbol.

It'd be a lot easier to cover this area if we split up, but I wasn't making that mistake again. We huddled together as we searched the circular room, but all we came across were shattered arrows and swords from years and years ago. They couldn't even be used as weapons anymore.

Then I looked more closely at the floor—and saw old blood!

No, that wasn't right. It was actually redstone in

the floor blocks. I let out a big sigh of relief. The red on the floor had sent my imagination racing, and I was thinking something outlandish, like that this was a place where a battle had happened. But why would a battle happen inside a jungle temple? There had to be a logical, non-scary answer to the red on the floor. And there would be a logical, non-scary answer to where Dad and Alex went. *This place isn't haunted*, I told myself.

I just wished I could shake off that evil feeling. It was the same feeling I got when the Ender Dragon spoke to me. I felt hate and anger and revenge and cruelty all rolled up in one. Like someone was telling me, *Get out of here. Get out of here before it's too late.*

And then I heard a voice in my mind.

You're in over your head, Stevie.

That voice, that evil voice!

Welcome to my home, the Ender Dragon continued. *To my old temple.*

I froze. *The claw marks!* I thought.

Yes, she said. *I made those.*

Get out of my head! I yelled at her silently. *I won't side with you, no matter what!*

The Ender Dragon didn't answer that. Instead, she changed the subject, her voice a low growl. *The villager was right: terrible things happened in this temple. And what a sense of humor he has, putting the shard here.*

He? I thought, confused. *You mean the villager?*

She gave a little snarl. *Don't be absurd! No villager could have done this.*

So "he" wasn't the villager. Then who was she talking about?

You don't need to worry about that right now, she said. *You don't know what's behind the next corner. That villager was wrong that there are armored ghosts here, but he's right that there are haunted guards. And I know you've noticed my Endermen. I'll be out of my prison soon enough. But* you *will never see daylight again.*

"Stop it!" I yelled, gripping my head. Everyone was staring at me, alarmed. Then I realized the Ender Dragon's voice was gone, and it was like a terrible weight had been lifted off me.

"It was the Ender Dragon!" I said, panting. "I'd hoped—I'd hoped—"

I'd hoped she'd finally leave me alone. I hadn't heard her awful voice since we'd returned home after finding the last crystal shard at Herobrine's temple, and I'd wanted to believe that meant she wouldn't haunt me anymore.

Haunt me. Maybe that wasn't the best choice of words.

"Oh, Stevie," Maison said, putting her hand on my shoulder. She had also heard the Ender Dragon's voice in the past, and knew its evil. But because she hadn't ever turned into an Enderman, the Ender Dragon's voice wasn't able to follow her like it had stuck with me.

I started to fill them in on the details. I hoped they couldn't see that my hands were shaking. And as I described it, I felt another haunting feeling come over me. It wasn't as bad as the feeling I got hearing the Ender Dragon, but it still sent a chill running up my spine.

I wasn't the only one to sense something bad.

"Oh no!" Destiny cried, looking behind us.

We whirled around. Three Endermen had joined us in the little room.

I opened my mouth to tell everyone to run, but it was too late. The Endermen had already spotted us, low growls coming from their throats like thunder. And then they were teleporting toward us.

CHAPTER 11

WITHOUT EVEN THINKING ABOUT TRAPS, WE dove through the nearest door, back onto the stage in the big, scary room. Which block had I stepped on to open all those doors? I needed to find it again so I could close them!

The others all had the same idea. Caution forgotten, we lunged from block to block, landing as hard as we could as if that would help. Blue hopped on a few blocks, too, looking proud of himself.

I hit on another block and I heard a noise. The doors were closing! I looked back just in time to see the doors close in the Endermen's faces. A second longer and they would have been able to teleport out into the room with us.

"Phew, that was close," Maison said.

"We're not safe yet. There are probably more," I said.

As soon as I said that, I heard the growl of an Enderman right next to me. I whirled with my diamond sword out, thinking one must have teleported at the last second and gotten out with us. But the creature my sword was pointed at wasn't a tall, menacing Enderman; it was Blue.

Blue looked at me funny and made the same growling sound I'd heard. I'd been so scared by that silly bird!

"Oh, so you can't repeat anything *I* tell you, but you can repeat monster sounds," Yancy said, still looking pale from our rush to safety. Blue flew over and settled back on Yancy's shoulder, ruffling his feathers as if he were pleased with himself.

"That's right," Maison said. "In the *Minecraft* game, parrots can mimic the sound of mobs."

Blue growled some more for effect and then fussed with his feathers happily. I felt my anger simmer. That bird had no idea what sort of danger we were all in!

"Let him go outside, Yancy," I said. "Set him free. He might cause problems for us. What if his noises lead more mobs our way?" Dad didn't think mobs would care about birds, but I didn't want to take any chances. We need to be as invisible to mobs as possible.

"I can't get rid of Blue," Yancy said. "He's part of the family now. And tamed parrots in *Minecraft* dance to jukebox music, which I am *dying* to see."

I eyed the bird. "Then just keep it quiet, please."

Yancy gave Blue another Oreo. At least the bird was silent as he gobbled the cookie down and sprayed crumbs everywhere. Then Blue let out another growl, though this time it sounded content.

Silly bird, I thought again. I'd always wanted a pet parrot myself, so if we weren't running from flying arrows and making our way around a (*haunted?*) jungle temple, I'd probably have enjoyed Blue's antics more. Right now I just wanted him to fly back into the jungle so we had one less thing to worry about.

We crept out of the creepy room and back into the hallway. It was time to go in the other direction. We kept close together, walking cautiously.

"I think I see trip wire," Maison said.

I held my torch out, and she was right. You could barely see the string in this lighting—it would have been hard to see even in daylight. But on each side of the wall there was a little indentation where the trip wire hooks were, and the string was attached to them. If we went walking straight though, arrows would fly out at us.

We ducked into the indentation to the side, which gave us just enough room, and moved the string enough that an arrow flew through the air right where we'd just been.

"I think I see where the source is too," Maison said, gesturing. A little farther down the hall there was a floating green bush. When I walked cautiously over and cut the bush away with my diamond sword, I saw the arrow dispenser. I quickly broke it and took its arrows. That meant at least this trip wire couldn't hurt us again!

"It's weird," Yancy said. "We got all the way down this hall, but I don't see any rooms. The other hallway had that big who-knows-what-happened-there room, and in this hall . . . nothing?"

"What are you saying?" Destiny asked.

"I'm saying there's no point in building a long hallway with nothing connected to it," Yancy said.

We all stood there and thought about it, until Blue began making skeleton sounds. Argh, that bird!

"Yancy, how many times do I have to tell you to keep that bird quiet?" I snapped.

"He is quiet," Yancy said.

I looked at Blue. He'd found his way into Yancy's backpack and was helping himself to whatever Earth food he was finding in there. The bird's beak was too full to be making any noises.

"Wait," I said, "does that mean . . ."

CHAPTER 12

SEVERAL ARMORED SKELETONS WERE STANDING right behind us, hissing. A hole in the wall had opened up, allowing them to sneak up on us from another hidden room.

Not only were the skeletons armored, they also had weapons! My eyes widened as I realized one of the skeletons was holding Alex's bow. Another skeleton let out a roar and lifted Dad's diamond sword about its head, shrieking in outrage.

Even though I couldn't speak skeleton like Blue could, I knew what that roar meant: *Get them!*

"Run!" Yancy said.

"No!" I said. "They have my dad's and Alex's weapons!"

I charged toward the skeleton holding Dad's sword,

striking at it with my own diamond sword. The skeleton roared again, pushing me back.

"These aren't armored ghosts!" Destiny exclaimed. "The haunted guards are *armored skeletons!*"

My friends dove for the skeletons, raising their own weapons. The skeleton with Alex's bow sent arrows flying at Maison, and she ducked and dove out of the way, barely dodging. In all the chaos Blue got knocked off Yancy's shoulder and flew away.

Destiny had to be right! The story must have evolved and changed over the years, so that it went from skeletons to ghosts. But this explained the skeletons on the warning sign outside the temple.

These skeletons got Dad and Alex! I thought, horrified and enraged. The monsters must have grabbed them and taken them somewhere. Skeletons will pick up better weapons if they're dropped, so they must have picked up Dad's and Alex's weapons when they got the chance!

"Give my dad and cousin back!" I hollered at the skeleton in front of me. Our swords clashed again, sending up blue sparks. "I know you have them!"

The skeleton hissed viciously in response, hitting me with its sword so hard it knocked me back. I wasn't down, though. I caught myself before I fell and charged the skeleton again.

The skeletons took this time to step completely out of the wall, and their door closed behind them. I never would have known there was a hidden door there because it looked like all the other mossy blocks in this temple.

I struck the skeleton I was fighting in the face with my sword, knocking off the armored helmet it wore. Then I hit it on the bare skull with my blade. I expected this to be a good hit, but it didn't faze the skeleton at all. I might as well have tapped it. Maybe that was why a story had spread that these skeletons were ghosts—they weren't as easy to damage as regular skeletons!

"I can't beat them!" Maison called, slashing with her sword. The others were protecting themselves and keeping the skeletons at bay, but they weren't able to weaken them any more than I was.

Maybe Yancy was right, and we should run. But what if that hidden door led to the dungeon the villager had warned us about, and Dad and Alex were being held there? Besides, I couldn't stand the thought of these evil mobs having weapons that rightfully belonged to Dad and Alex!

The guards have found you, Stevie, the Ender Dragon mocked.

Not her! Not now!

She continued, *They have one mission: to protect this temple from outsiders. Outsiders like you and your family.*

Leave me alone! I shouted at her, trying to concentrate on the skeleton in front of me.

Bow to me, she ordered. *Bow to me and you will be saved. Your father and cousin are already gone. But I can make everything better. I'm the only one who can.*

I sucked in an angry, trembling breath. Even though she was evil, her voice sometimes had a soothing quality, like letting go and allowing darkness to surround you like a blanket. It was wrong and it was frightening, but it also meant I could just stop fighting. Just stop fighting and surrender to her.

No! I yelled. *My dad and Alex are still safe! I'm going to find them and rescue them!*

Only one man has ever escaped here, the Ender Dragon said. *And you do not have his skills. You will fail.*

Her words made me so angry I felt full of energy, like a redstone current. I hit the skeleton with all my might, hoping to knock Dad's sword out of its bony hands. The skeleton didn't even waver, but the force of my swing left my legs unsteady.

The skeleton easily struck me back with Dad's sword, throwing me to the ground.

CHAPTER 13

MAISON JUMPED IN FRONT OF ME, HOLDING out her sword. "Don't even think about it!" she told the skeleton.

This gave me time to scramble back to my feet. The ground was slick with moss, making it harder for me to get up.

That's when the hidden door opened again. I looked over, hoping against hope that Dad and Alex would show up. But it was more armored skeletons with their own swords and arrows.

A rain of arrows shot at me and I dodged, rolling across the ground. When I got back up, I was dizzy but unhurt. Quickly I turned, charging back into the fight.

"There are too many of them!" Yancy shouted. "We need to retreat!"

"They'll just chase us!" I argued.

There was movement from the darkness on the other side of the hidden door. More skeletons were coming out. In the torchlight, their teeth gleamed in wide, morbid smiles of destruction.

I realized I couldn't argue with Yancy anymore. I didn't know what to do. "All right, let's go!" I said.

We took off racing down the dark hall, the skeletons at our heels. I looked out a window as we passed it and saw several Endermen just outside the temple, hunting for the shard on the steps. That meant we couldn't go back outside. We were surrounded by mobs!

We could run down the stairs, but that would trap us in the little room again. We could run into the room with the claw marks, but we'd be trapped there too. If we went through the trap door at the back of the stage, that would just put us back with more Endermen. There was no way out. What were we going to do?

The only thing I could think of was to go upstairs, to the third floor of the temple. We hadn't been there before and didn't know what to expect. Would there be more armored skeletons? Would there be a way out?

Would Dad and Alex be there?

"Upstairs!" I called to the others. "It's our only chance!"

Behind us, a skeleton let out a roar that seemed to shake the whole temple. And then Destiny screamed.

I froze in my spot and whirled around. In our

hurry, we weren't checking for traps, and her foot had landed on a trapdoor in the floor. That block had opened up and she'd fallen halfway through. Her chest and upper shoulders were still out, and she was trying frantically to pull herself back up. But the flat, mossy blocks around her were too slick for her to get a good grip.

"Destiny!" I cried, turning back.

A skeleton reared over Destiny, only to have a sword smashed into its face as Yancy came running to the rescue. Maison joined him in battle, and together they kept the skeletons from reaching Destiny.

"Hurry, Destiny!" Yancy said. "We can't hold them off much longer!"

They were barely keeping them back at all. I realized the best thing would be to pull Destiny to safety and then run again. I lunged down to the floor next to the trapdoor.

"Destiny, take my hand!" I said, reaching out.

She put one hand out, but then a skeleton shot an arrow past Yancy and Destiny. I had to yank my own hand back as I dove out of the way. Destiny was already balancing with only one hand, and the arrow startled her so much she lost her grip. She let out another scream as she slipped farther into the hole.

"No!" I ducked forward, dodging another arrow. "Destiny!"

Her fingers were curled around the edge of the

hole, but the rest of her was hanging down into the darkness. I had to drop the torch to the ground so I could grab her hands and look down at her. Even in the dark hollow of the hole, I could see how white her face had gone in her terror.

"Stevie, help me!" she begged.

"I am! I am!" I said. But the skeletons with bows and arrows had seen that I was in a weak spot and decided to make me target practice. Arrows were flying all around me. One even zigged right past my shoulder, ripping a hole in my turquoise shirt.

"Destiny, pull yourself up!" I said, struggling to keep my grip on her. I couldn't hold her weight and dodge arrows at the same time!

"I'm trying!" she said desperately. Her feet were hitting against the rock wall of the tunnel, but she couldn't get a foothold.

"Oh no!" I cried, throwing myself to the side before an arrow could hit me. The arrow landed exactly where I'd been, quivering as it embedded itself into the floor.

That split second move to save myself was enough to ruin it all for Destiny. I'd needed to let go of her to move, and without my hands, she lost her grip.

With a scream, she plummeted into the darkness, the floor closing up behind her.

CHAPTER 14

"**D**ESTINY, NOOO!" I EXCLAIMED, HITTING THE floor with my hands, trying to get the trap-door to open back up. It wouldn't budge!

"What happened?" Yancy said, turning around, his eyes wild with fear. The scream and the cries must have given him a pretty good idea.

"She fell through!" I said, panicking.

"Then we're going with her," Yancy said, throwing himself on the trapdoor. At least if we were still with Destiny, we could make sure she was okay and we'd all find a way out together. But the trapdoor wouldn't open for Yancy, either.

Maison couldn't keep the skeletons away on her own, and I saw they were overpowering her. If we didn't do something, the skeletons would snatch all three of us!

"Keep running!" I said, even though it hurt to say that. I seized the torch from where it was lying on the floor. I told myself I wasn't leaving Destiny behind. I was just keeping us safe so we could come back for her. "We need to go upstairs!"

Yancy started to argue, but Maison didn't.

"How could you let her fall!" Yancy was shouting at me. I'd never seen him so upset. I knew he and Destiny were close because they were cousins, but Yancy looked ready to fall apart because of this. I realized, for the first time, just how much they meant to each other.

"I didn't mean to!" I said.

"Stop it, Yancy!" Maison defended. "We already have to rescue Alex and Steve! We'll rescue Destiny too!"

But Yancy still looked like he'd fight me if we didn't already have other problems. "I trusted you, Stevie!" he snarled.

I was already feeling terrible—I didn't need Yancy rubbing it in. I snapped back, "What about you, Yancy? You're the one going on about coconuts and bringing a noisy bird along and talking about the temple being haunted. How have you been helpful?"

"You think skeletons that can't be defeated *aren't* haunted?" Yancy shot back.

I knew it was just our emotions running high because we were so stressed, so I bit back a nasty response to Yancy. An arrow whizzed past my ear, reminding me there were more important things to pay attention to right now.

Besides, we were coming up to the sets of stairs again. Out of the corner of my eye I noticed the torch by the front door had moved again. Was that the skeletons' doing? Maison, Yancy, and I ran upstairs, the skeletons hissing at our heels, arrows flying. Someone kicked a trip wire and arrows soared straight toward our faces, making us all duck. I spilled backward down the stairs, almost losing hold of my sword and torch.

Something grabbed my leg.

I looked back wildly. The skeleton with Dad's sword had seized my ankle in its bony hand. The hand felt cold as ice while it gripped me. Then the skeleton began to raise Dad's sword.

There was no escape now.

CHAPTER 15

I TRIED TO ANGLE MYSELF TO STRIKE BACK, BUT there wasn't time. Yancy jumped in the way, hitting the skeleton with his sword, forcing it back. The skeleton lost its balance and fell backward, knocking into the other skeletons behind it. Unsteady on the old mossy steps, the skeletons tumbled to the bottom of the stairs.

I tried to give Yancy a grateful look, but he was too busy grabbing my hand and hoisting me to my feet. He didn't even look in my eyes, as if he was embarrassed for getting so mad at me earlier.

I pushed myself up onto my feet with Yancy's help and took a quick look behind me. The skeletons had been startled, but definitely not stopped. They were already rising back up on their feet, shaking themselves off, and getting ready to come after us again. I could have sworn the one with Dad's sword was glaring at me, as if vowing revenge.

Maison, Yancy, and I scrambled to the top of the stairs and looked around us. Like on the floor below, we saw a dark hallway sprawling in both directions. I didn't see any rooms, and if there were any trapdoors, it wasn't obvious. I ran to the closest window and looked down. Could we jump to safety?

The ground below looked so far down it made me dizzy. That wasn't even the worst part of it. Even if we slowly climbed our way down the temple, it wouldn't be any sort of a real escape, because the jungle out there was now swarming with Endermen. They had the whole temple surrounded.

"There's no way out," I said.

Maison began pounding her fists against the walls. "Open up!" she said. "There has to be a hidden door here somewhere!"

She was probably right, but who had time to find any hidden doors? And even if we found one, where would it lead us? To more skeletons? To the dungeon? To an army of Endermen?

What would Dad do? I thought frantically. *What would Alex do?*

Then, *What would Steve Alexander do?*

I had no idea. There was only what Stevie, Maison, and Yancy would do, and we were running out of options. Fast.

Then I saw something out of the corner of my eye. The light of my torch was shining on a block in the wall that looked different from all the other walls here. What was it?

I laid my hand against it. More claw marks. Claw marks raked several times over, as if trying to erase something. But there was more! Underneath all the claw marks I could make out the letters S and A. The fancy symbol of Steve Alexander.

A clue! I began whacking my sword against the wall and floor in that area, seeing if anything would open up. Maison and Yancy saw what I was doing and rushed to join me.

"Come on, come on! We could use a hidden door any time now," Yancy said. He dared a glance over his shoulder at the same time I did. The skeletons were reaching the top of the stairway now. The torchlight made their empty eye sockets look as if they were filled with red flame. And they looked angrier than ever.

I pounded harder on the wall, begging for something to give through. Clues weren't any good if we couldn't figure out what they meant!

For a split second I thought I saw some other writing underneath the claw marks, after the S A symbol. It looked like . . . like the letter J. And maybe a . . . no, I couldn't tell what the letter was after that, but I could tell it used to say more than just J there.

Steve Alexander and J, again! Why didn't any of

the legends or Steve Alexander's book mention a J, or a J name?

The skeletons came charging toward us, forcing us to move away from the mysterious marks. I turned and slashed out at the mobs, trying to keep them at bay. I saw a blade rushing at me the same time a slew of arrows flew in my direction. I leapt to the side, falling into the hole of an open window. My hands were holding the torch and my sword, and I couldn't hold both and grab onto the ledge! I was going to tumble out!

While I barely managed to hang on, my eyes fell to the drop below. We were above the treetops here, and a rush of dizziness flooded my head. The Endermen were still unaware of me, but if I fell, I'd land right in the middle of their crowd, right in their clutches.

I had to drop my sword or my torch. Which one? Without my sword, I wouldn't have a weapon. Without my torch, we wouldn't have any real light!

"I got you, Stevie!" It was Maison's voice, and she grabbed me around the middle and started pulling me back into the temple. My head swung over open air, and then I felt myself being pulled back into the dank, dark building. Back to danger and safety.

As soon as Maison had gotten me back on my feet, she cried out. An arrow had slashed past her, going straight through her hair and ripping out a few black strands. Maison fell to a crouch. She wasn't really hurt, but that must have scared her, especially with the arrow coming so close to her head.

I turned to Yancy. But it was already too late.

CHAPTER 16

WHILE MAISON HAD BEEN TRYING TO RESCUE me, Yancy had been left all alone to fight off the approaching skeletons. He hadn't been able to do it. But instead of taking him out, the skeletons had surrounded him so that there was no escape. Then four of the skeletons grabbed his arms, forcing them down to his side. Another skeleton ripped the sword out of Yancy's hand.

Yancy was trying to fight as hard as he could, swinging his body back and forth so they'd let him go. It didn't make any difference. More skeletons came out of the woodwork and grabbed him. They were like spiders covering him with web, holding him tighter and tighter until he couldn't move. Until he couldn't breathe.

"Yancy!" I said, running toward him. Yancy was

lurching backward like a frightened horse, and the skeletons still held him in place. The only skeleton who wasn't touching him was the one with Dad's diamond sword. That skeleton strode proudly forward, silently gloating. It held Dad's sword straight out toward Yancy, as though daring him to try anything.

Yancy stopped struggling and his eyes widened when he saw the sword. He licked his lips nervously and said, "Hey, guys, come on. We don't want your jungle temple. Just give us back the others, let us take the crystal shard, and we'll leave you alone forever. I promise."

I guess he was hoping that, if these skeletons were haunted, they might also have the ability to understand us. But whether the skeletons understood him or not, their expressions didn't change. The skeleton with Dad's sword let out a commanding roar, and the others began dragging Yancy down the long hallway.

"Stop it!" I cried as I reached the skeleton with Dad's sword and struck it over the head with my blade. In response, the skeleton turned and gave me such sharp wallop with its sword that it sent me flying across the room. I landed hard against the wall, choking and coughing. The skeleton with Dad's sword gestured for another skeleton to go after me and it obeyed, slowly stalking my way.

It was all up to Maison to save Yancy now. She went charging in too, running past the skeleton I'd gone after and heading straight for the horde that had Yancy.

"Let him go!" she shouted, slashing at them. A few skeletons took their hands off of Yancy to fight back, but it wasn't enough. Instead, those two skeletons grabbed Maison, too, and tried to take her sword.

No! I couldn't let that happen! I was back on my feet and charging toward them, slashing with my sword. I hit the skeleton coming at me, pushing it to the side. One of the skeletons picked up Maison as if she weighed nothing and threw her out the window.

Suddenly, it was like time slowed down. Maison grabbed onto the window with her fingers, struggling to hold on, clawing her way back up, scrambling for hold with her feet. I had a flashback to Destiny's fall. Not again!

I ran to the window and grabbed Maison's hands, even though it meant putting down my sword and torch for a moment. I had to use both hands this time. I had to get her back up!

Something icy cold grabbed me around the waist. A skeleton! Another was running to grab my torch and sword. In the background, the other skeletons were dragging Yancy farther away.

"Let go!" I cried, as though there was any hope that the skeleton would listen. It was trying to drag me away, to take me wherever it was taking Yancy! It was trying to let Maison fall below, to the Endermen who would take her as their own prisoner!

But then my eyes caught on something. There was

a little ledge underneath Maison, where she could land without falling all the way down to the ground where the Endermen were.

"Maison!" I said. "I have to let you drop!"

"No, Stevie, don't!" she called back.

"There's a ledge below you!" I said. "Land there and I'll be right back!"

I let her hands slip from mine. Maison's eyes were full of fear, but also determination. She curled herself up into a ball and fell down onto the ledge, landing there safely.

I turned my back to the window, striking at the skeletons that were trying to take my sword and torch. As soon as they backed up slightly, I grabbed my weapon and light.

I needed to get to Yancy. But there was no way I could take out so many skeletons on my own!

Down the hall, I saw the skeleton with Dad's sword touch its bony hand against the wall. Immediately a door opened, showing only darkness beyond. The skeleton walked through, and the skeletons holding Yancy began to follow.

"No!" Yancy was shouting, fighting harder, realizing he was really on his own now. "Stop, stop, pleeeease!"

It was no use. The skeletons forced him through that hidden door, into the darkness, and followed behind him so he couldn't get out. I caught one last glimpse of their weapons, shining in the torchlight. And then the door shut, cutting off Yancy's screams for help.

CHAPTER 17

THE REMAINING SKELETONS HAD ME TRAPPED AT the window. I couldn't go forward with them pressed against me like that, and they were trying to grab me and take my weapon.

You're all alone now, Stevie, the Ender Dragon said. *Give in to me.*

"Stevie!" I heard Maison shouting from below. "Stevie, what's going on?"

No! I thought. *I'm not alone! I still have Maison.*

An Earth girl can't save you!

Then you don't know Maison, I thought. *And you don't know me.*

And I threw myself out the window.

The wind was whipping up all around me, the ground a long way below. I tried to shut my mind off from the Ender Dragon. Maison and I had been friends long before Destiny and Yancy came into the picture. Before I really got to know and befriend my cousin Alex. Maison and I had stopped a mob attack at her school on our own. We'd stopped cyberbullies from plunging the Overworld into eternal darkness. As long as I had Maison, I was not alone!

I landed on the ledge next to Maison. The crash was startling but not painful.

"Stevie!" Maison knelt beside me. "Are you all right?"

I didn't answer right away, because I didn't know. This was a gamble. I looked up at the windowsill and saw two skeletons peering down at us. Were they going to jump out the window and follow us?

No. After looking at us a few seconds, the skeleton faces moved away from the window.

"I was right," I sighed, feeling a moment of relief. "They only want to protect the temple. As long as we're not in it, they'll leave us alone."

"Where's Yancy?" Maison asked.

That took away any relief I was feeling. I shut my eyes and could still hear Yancy's screams in my head. First I'd let them take Dad, Alex, Destiny, and now Yancy.

"They dragged him through a hidden door in the wall," I said, horrified even as I was saying it.

Maison clapped her hands over her mouth, alarmed. "No!"

"We have to get back inside there somehow," I said. "We have to rescue them."

I saw from Maison's face that she was trying to figure out what to do. "We've been to all the main rooms," she said. "So they have to be in a hidden room somewhere."

"Who knows how many hidden rooms there are, though?" I said. This was a much harder crystal-shard mission than the ones before. "And how do we find the triggers to open the doors?"

"We could wait until daylight," Maison said. "Then the skeletons should be gone."

I wasn't so sure. It was a really dank, dark place in that temple, so it might be dark enough for them to still be around during the day. Then I looked down at the Endermen. Even if the skeletons would be gone, the Endermen could stick around in light. We couldn't let them find the crystal shard before us!

"I have an idea!" Maison suddenly said. "We haven't explored the basement much. We can go back to that little room downstairs and start knocking out blocks to see if we find hidden rooms."

That could be time-consuming, but it might also work. "Yeah," I said. "Because it's a big building and we could only see a little bit of the downstairs, so there have to be more rooms there."

"How do we get there?" Maison asked.

That . . . was a good question. I looked up at the window. "Do you have a bow and arrow?" I asked.

She did, though she didn't usually use it since Alex was the best archer around. Maison reached into her toolkit and pulled out a bow and arrow she'd made. I took a lead out of my toolkit, tied the arrow off, and shot it through the window. It landed somewhere, and I tested the line to make sure it was strong enough to hold both of our weight.

As long as the skeletons had gone away completely, we would be able to get back inside through the window. I hadn't heard any skeleton noises, so it was worth a chance. If I climbed back up and there were still skeletons, I could drop back down to the ledge and rethink plans.

"Follow me," I said, handing Maison back the bow and arrows. I also gave her the torch so I could hold my sword and still have a hand open for climbing.

We began slowly making our away up the lead. I looked at the sky, hoping to see a little bit of gray on the horizon signaling that it was almost dawn and we might get some relief. But there was no sign the sun was coming up soon.

When I got up to the window, I peeked through with just the top of my head above the sill. I couldn't see any danger directly ahead of me.

"How does it look?" Maison whispered from below.

I pulled myself up a little more and looked to the

left and then to the right. The hallway was silent and empty.

"It looks good," I whispered back, then scrambled the rest of the way up. A moment later Maison followed.

"Where was the hidden door they took Yancy through?" she asked.

"Uh . . ." I racked my brain. I knew the general area where the skeleton had touched the wall, but I couldn't tell her the exact block that had opened the door. "It's somewhere around here."

"Well, we might as well at least try to open it and find Yancy that way," she said.

We began knocking along the wall, and I wondered if this was a good idea. It might lead us to Yancy faster, or it could turn us into sitting ducks (an Earth phrase I learned from Yancy) and the skeletons would find us before we ever reached the basement and tried out our plan.

When a skeleton hissed just behind my neck, I got my answer.

CHAPTER 18

I WHIPPED AROUND, SWORD OUT. IT WAS ONLY BLUE!
"You silly bird!" I said, but I was so relieved. Blue
sang out some more skeleton sounds, looking happy
as can be.

Maison touched some more blocks in the wall and
then sighed. "This isn't working. Let's go downstairs."

We made our way down the steps with Blue floating
along beside us, chirping and mimicking the skeletons.

"I wish we could make him quiet," I said.

"Maybe this is what Yancy gets for feeding it cookies instead of seeds," Maison said. "That parrot is on a
sugar rush."

"Yeah," I said. "When we get out of here, we'll need
to find it some seeds."

If you get out of there, the Ender Dragon chose to
remind me. *Which you won't.*

Down the dark steps we went. I could see the big entrance to the temple, and thankfully there still weren't any skeletons. Had they all returned to their hidden rooms?

The better question is, the Ender Dragon told me, *what are they doing to your family and friends?*

I sucked in a harsh breath. Maison said, "Stevie, what is it?"

Before I could answer, Blue let out an especially loud skeleton sound. I turned to shush the bird, but instead I saw several skulls staring at me from the stairwell leading down into the basement. It was the real thing!

The next second, the skeletons were running toward us, hissing. I spotted the ones with Dad's sword and Alex's arrow, but Yancy wasn't with them. Where had they taken him?

"Run!" I said. But where was there to run? Maison and I raced down the hallway.

We both stumbled over something at the same time. Another trip wire! Arrows shot straight at us, but we had fallen forward, so they went right over our heads. I glanced back for an instant and saw the arrows hit two skeletons instead. The skeletons jolted for an instant, but that was it. They weren't hurt. They kept marching forward, coming after us.

Blue was flying with us, mixing up his sounds with happy chirps and angry skeleton growls. Boy, I wanted to chuck that bird out the window!

But, wait . . . no! What was I thinking? Here I was so mad at the bird, when Blue could be our way out of all this!

"Blue!" I shouted as we ran. "Where's Yancy? Where's the boy who feeds you?"

Still flying, Blue looked my way with his head tilted, as if trying to understand me.

Maison realized what I was doing. When animals like parrots are tamed, they will always seek out the person who tamed them. They know how to find the person who feeds them!

"Find Yancy, Blue!" Maison said. "He'll give you more Oreos!"

Maybe it was the mention of cookies, but Blue suddenly turned in the other direction.

No! He was leading us back toward the skeletons!

Maison and I looked at each other. We had no choice. If that was the direction Yancy, Dad, Alex, and Destiny were in, we had to follow!

"Ready?" I asked.

"I'm always ready," she said.

We turned to the skeletons, our weapons out. "Just get past them and follow Blue!" I said.

But Maison was already ahead of me. We slashed around the skeletons, dodging them when they tried to grab us. One caught Maison by her shirt, holding her in place. I slashed with my sword again and the skeleton released her. The skeletons seemed surprised that we'd stopped running and were coming back. It was almost like we caught them off-guard.

Soon after we ran past the skeletons, Blue stopped flying a little way ahead of us, and he landed on the floor. Was that a clue? Parrots also stopped flying when they were tired. What if Blue didn't know what he was doing, and he'd just gotten us trapped by skeletons?

The skeletons were following, gaining on us. One reached out and seized my shirt in its bony hands. I hit its arm with my blade and the skeleton pulled back, ripping part of my shirt. I could still feel the skeleton's icy cold touch against my skin, even after its hand had fallen away.

When Maison and I were seconds away from Blue, he hopped back in the air, hovering above the place where he had landed. What was going on? My foot struck the block Blue had been on, and then I had my answer. The floor opened up beneath me, showing a stretch of darkness below. Maison was right behind me, and as soon as I started to fall, she started to fall with me. We both plunged down into the hole, with Blue gliding down after us. At first all I saw was a flash of navy blue and the skeletons watching us from overhead. Then the trapdoor sealed off and we fell down and down and landed on a dirt floor.

I let out a groan and slowly sat up. What had happened? Where were we?

Maison was also lifting herself up, and she raised the torch so we could see.

We were in an enormous room full of cages and prison cells, with shackles chained to the wall and absolutely no sunlight coming in.

I let out a low gulp.

Blue had taken us to the temple's dungeon.

CHAPTER 19

"HELLO?" I CALLED, HOPING SOMEONE WOULD answer. "Is anybody there?"

"Stevie, is that you?" Dad's voice called.

I was so relieved my heart almost stopped. Maison and I pulled ourselves to our feet and ran down the hall, with Blue leading the way. I heard Alex, Yancy, and Destiny calling to us too.

As we ran, our torch lit more of the room. So far all the cages and cells we'd passed were empty, and that was a good thing. I couldn't imagine being stuck in one of those!

Finally Blue stopped flying and hovered in the air. Right in front of him were Dad, Alex, Destiny, and Yancy, each in their own little cell.

"Stevie, Maison!" Dad said. "Thank goodness you've found us!"

"Are you hurt?" I cried.

"No," Dad said. The others shook their heads.

"I was waiting for the trapdoor to open, and the next thing I knew, I was surrounded by skeleton guards," Dad went on. "They knocked me down and took my sword before I could respond."

I was amazed. The skeletons had to have been really sneaky to slip up on Dad like that!

"They grabbed me, touched the wall, and opened up a door," Dad went on. "By the time they got me through the door and sealed it off, I had realized what was happening and was calling out for you. But you must not have heard."

"The same thing happened to me," Alex said. She didn't look scared—she looked piping mad! "I broke through the wall and then these stupid skeletons grabbed me and took my bow and arrows. They opened a door in the wall and dragged me down this tunnel and into this dungeon. No one is allowed to use my bow and arrows!"

"Are the skeletons here?" I asked, my eyes darting around. I couldn't see any, but they could have been preparing to slip out of the darkness and into the torchlight.

"I don't think so," Dad said. "Each time they bring another one of us here, they leave to search for more."

"They just want us out of the temple, Dad," I said. "I think as soon as we're out, they'll stop chasing us."

"Is there anyone else in this dungeon?" Maison asked.

"No," Dad said. "Just us. I've been trying to find a way to escape."

I looked at the cell doors. Did they have keyholes? I didn't see any, and I didn't know where the keys would be, anyway—maybe carried around by the skeletons? No, there had to be another way.

Blue squeezed himself through the bars and perched on Yancy's left shoulder.

"Hey, Blue, my man," Yancy said. "I thought I'd never see you again."

"He's the one who led us here," Maison said.

"Aww, does that mean you like me?" Yancy said, sounding touched.

In response, Blue tried to dive into Yancy's backpack for more food. Yancy gently pulled him out, but Blue was already eating something.

"Maybe Blue can also lead us out of the temple," Maison said.

I frowned. First, we needed to get everyone out of their cells.

"Maison, can I have the torch for a second?" I asked.

"Sure." She handed it back, looking at me. I knew she was trying to figure out what I was thinking.

I was thinking I needed to explore more of this dungeon, in case there were clues. Maybe there was a switch somewhere that would let everyone out. Or maybe I could find a better weapon to break open the cell doors. Maison realized what I was doing, and she began searching the walls as well.

I made my way through the dungeon very carefully, moving the torch along the walls. I kept revealing more and more cells. They all looked nasty and lonesome. The bars created shadows along the mossy walls that made the room feel like one big, giant cage to trap us all in.

I didn't see any exits. And I definitely wasn't seeing any keys. Or clues.

Then the strangest thing happened. Out of nowhere, the Ender Dragon let out a sharp sound in my head. It wasn't a word. It was like she was reacting to something, and the sound was somewhere between a painful sigh and a harsh intake of breath—like the sound someone would make if they were startled by something that made them feel angry.

This stopped me in my tracks. What would make the Ender Dragon react like that? I waited a moment, but she didn't make any more noises. It was almost like something got to her, and now she was quiet, really quiet.

On the far wall was a cell that was bigger than all the other cells. The shadows it cast looked barbed, as though the walls were made of teeth, ready to bite. It'd gotten rusty over the years, and the door hung open a little. There was a sign on top of the cell.

When I raised my torch to read the sign, I made my own startled sound without realizing it.

The sign said, THIS CELL IS HOME TO THE PRISONER STEVE ALEXANDER.

CHAPTER 20

"**N**O WAY!" I EXCLAIMED. I THREW OPEN THE cell door, listening as it groaned on its rusty hinges.

My thoughts were galloping faster than a wild horse. *Something terrible happened here . . . bad enchantments . . . haunted . . . a dungeon . . . Steve Alexander's cell!*

Maison had hurried over. She read the sign and asked, "Was Steve Alexander put in prison for some reason?"

"No!" I said. "I mean, not that I ever heard of! But . . . but . . ."

What had happened here? Why were there claw marks on the walls? Why did the Ender Dragon say this was her home and her temple? Had Steve Alexander been a prisoner of the Ender Dragon before he made her *his* prisoner and put her in the End?

I realized that, as much as I wanted to get out of this temple, it must hold really important clues to the past. This wasn't just the home of a crystal shard. Steve Alexander was also trying to tell me what had happened centuries ago. But all the details were running around in my head and I couldn't connect them.

"What's going on?" Alex called from her cell.

Maison shouted back, telling her what we'd found, and Alex replied that Steve Alexander was never in prison, no way, no how, not our ancestor, the hero Steve Alexander. Alex would not accept the idea that Steve Alexander had any human failings. Steve Alexander may have been imprisoned by an evil dragon trying to stop him from doing good, but that was still just weakness to Alex. (Never mind the fact she was shouting this from her *own* prison cell.)

They say only one man has ever been able to escape from that dungeon, the villager had said, and I thought I had a feeling who that one man had been. When I was inside the cell, I tried to think of what it would be like to be Steve Alexander, trapped in here. The doors slamming shut, keeping freedom out. The long bars. The evil dragon as your captor. It made me shiver.

And why was there a sign saying this was Steve Alexander's cell? None of the other cells had signs, let alone signs with names. Was the Ender Dragon trying to humiliate him? Or trying to show off that she'd captured the one and only Steve Alexander?

There was debris on the floor, and I squatted down and pushed it to the side. My heart gave another leap. Someone had sketched the letters S and A on the floor. It wasn't as neat as Steve Alexander's symbol usually was, but maybe he'd carved this while a prisoner, using whatever tools he could find.

I began hitting the ground with my diamond sword, breaking through the blocks. I heard Maison say my name, but it was like someone was talking to me while I was underwater. I was fully concentrated on what I was doing.

I knocked away a few more blocks, and then I saw a purple glow from down below. The violet light filled the whole cell and made it feel more magical and less frightening.

I dove my hand in and pulled out the crystal shard.

CHAPTER 21

"**I** FOUND IT, I FOUND IT!" I EXCLAIMED.

"Yes!" Maison cheered. "And Stevie, look! I found a switch."

She touched something on the wall, and all the other cell doors popped open.

Dad, Alex, Destiny, and Yancy ran gratefully out of their cells. Destiny tried to give Yancy a hug, but he was too busy stretching his long limbs and cracking something. Yancy had been so concerned about Destiny earlier, and now he was acting so cool about it. But I knew the truth. Blue whistled and chirped happily.

"Now let's get our weapons back and get out of here!" Alex said.

"Forget the weapons," Dad said. "We can always make ourselves new ones. We don't want to mess with those skeleton guards again."

Alex pouted but didn't argue.

Dad went up to one of the walls and put his hands on it. "Now, I know we came through a trapdoor around here somewhere," he said. "If we find that trapdoor, it will take us to the entrance so we can get out."

Glad to have found the crystal shard at last, I tucked it safely into my toolkit. Then I joined the others, checking along the wall for the switch. Hopefully Steve Alexander's book would help solve the rest of the mysteries about the jungle temple. In the meantime, I was ready to go home!

Still sitting on Yancy's left shoulder, Blue began making skeleton sounds.

"Shh, Blue," Yancy said. "That's not the kind of stuff I want you repeating. You're going to scare us all."

Blue kept making the noise, staring at one part of the wall. That was weird, because now that he was tame, normally Blue stared at whatever Yancy stared at. But the parrot's eyes would not leave that one spot.

That's when the wall parted where Blue was looking, showing a doorframe with just blackness on the other side of it.

Good bird! I thought. Maybe he really did know the way out, and that's why he was staring at where the hidden door was!

We all started to take a step forward, then froze. It wasn't just darkness after all. Something was moving right past the doorframe. Something tall and white, like moonlight. I heard a hiss, and this time it wasn't coming from Blue. It was coming from the darkness.

The skeleton guards stepped through the doorframe, blocking our only exit.

CHAPTER 22

"IT'S THEM AGAIN!" ALEX YELLED FIERCELY, HER EYES full of anger.

"Charge them!" Dad said. "All we need to do is get past them and out of the temple!"

The skeleton with Dad's sword let out a terrifying roar, shaking its skull head. Then our two groups rushed at each other.

I went straight for the skeleton with Dad's sword. I especially hated that thief!

Our two swords clashed, making blue sparks fly. My face was inches from the skeleton's as we both strained with our weapons. The empty hollows where its eyes would have been were staring at me with black intensity like the deepest part of night.

Dad came up and struck the skeleton in the skull with his fist. Even barehanded, Dad was a great fighter.

It startled the skeleton long enough that I pulled back my sword and thrust it again, knocking Dad's sword out of the skeleton's grasp. The sword went flying through the air, did a spin, and landed right in Dad's ready hand.

"Thanks, Stevie!" Dad said.

Before I could answer, I felt an arrow whizz by my chest, almost ripping my already-torn shirt. I looked and saw that the skeleton that had shot at me was the one with Alex's bow and arrows. *Might as well right this wrong too,* I thought, running toward the skeleton. It pulled back Alex's bow and sent an arrow straight toward me. But I put my sword up so that the arrow hit my blade and bounced off instead.

The next second I was on the skeleton, hitting the bow out of its hands. Alex dove forward and grabbed her bow. She still had some arrows in her toolkit, and she ripped them out and set them on the bow's string, aiming for the skeleton.

"Hey, remember me?" she snapped. "Don't take things that don't belong to you!"

"Kids, follow me!" Dad said. He pushed through the skeletons, knocking several of them to the side. We all raced after him, following his path through the horde. A skeleton grabbed me on my way and I emitted a startled choking sound. Dad turned, eyes full of fury, and struck the skeleton with his sword, forcing it to release me.

We made it past the skeletons, but now we were in a dark, empty hallway, and the skeletons were at our heels. They wanted to take us back to the dungeon.

"Which way?" Maison shouted.

"Blue, which way out?" Yancy said. Blue hopped off Yancy's shoulder and flew ahead of us, so we all followed him. The hallway was tightly closed in now, so we could barely move except in single file. That forced the skeletons farther back, though it still meant they were just behind us.

We came to a dead end.

"Find whatever triggers the hidden door!" Dad said.

We all began pounding the walls, trying to find a switch or trigger or something. Yancy let out a cry. He was the last person in line, and a skeleton had grabbed him again.

Blue turned at the sound of the cry and flew back, landing on the skeleton's skull and pecking at it. The skeleton tried to push the bird away but fell back instead, ramming into the other skeletons behind it.

"Got it!" Destiny said, hitting something. There was a sliver of light as the wall in front of us opened up. We all rushed to get through the doorway so fast that we ended up tripping over one another and almost spilled out on the floor. Catching ourselves, we got through the doorway.

"Close the door!" Dad said.

"I don't know how!" Destiny said. "Besides, they know how to open it!"

Dad grunted, because Destiny was right. I could see the entrance of the temple to our right, and our torch was still placed by it, though it had been moved again. But who cared about that? Here was our exit!

We ran toward it, the skeletons following. But something was different now. The entrance and the windows were showing soft, buttery light. It was dawn!

When the skeletons reached the first window, they stopped. The light hurt them, causing them to smoke. They could handle our weapons, just not sunlight! One by one the skeletons drew back into the darkness to protect themselves.

Yes! I thought. *We made it! We made it!*

But, just then, I heard the Ender Dragon's evil laughter in my head. The area in front of the jungle temple was crawling with even more Endermen than before. And when I reached the entrance, with my toolkit glowing purple from the crystal shard, the Endermen all looked my way.

CHAPTER 23

"**A**WW, MAN," YANCY SAID, FREEZING BESIDE ME. "This is just the night that doesn't end."

He was right. Because even though it didn't count as night anymore, the dawn wasn't going to protect us from Endermen. We had to come up with an idea, and it had to be quick!

The Endermen began teleporting toward us. Moments ago they had been in the bushes nearby, and now they were reaching the temple steps.

Time's up, Stevie, the Ender Dragon said. *It was very entertaining watching you tonight, but we both knew how this would end.*

"Run upstairs!" Dad shouted, and we followed after him. I didn't even know why. I just needed directions right then. Dad must have thought that going upstairs would give us another way out, because he hadn't been up there. But I had, and I knew better.

When we got to the top floor, Dad ran directly to the first window. I was right behind him. We both looked out and saw a devastating sight: there were even more Endermen below the window than we had seen from the entrance. Almost every block of grass had its own Enderman standing on top of it.

"Maybe we can hide in one of the secret rooms," Yancy said.

"So the skeletons can get us again?" Destiny cried.

Pick your poison, Stevie, the Ender Dragon said. *Do you want to be captured by the skeletons who guard my haunted temple, or by my own Enderman soldiers?*

As she was saying that, Blue flew out the window and landed on a nearby treetop. He turned back and looked at us as if he were expecting something.

Blue has it, I realized. *Blue is right!*

"We can escape on the treetops!" I said. "We'll be high enough above the Endermen that they won't see us. Endermen have a hard time teleporting to treetops!"

Dad's eyes lit up. "You're right. But how do we get there?"

"Like this!" Maison said, already understanding. She leapt out the window.

"Maison, no!" Destiny said.

"It's all right!" Maison called from the ledge below. She had landed on her feet and was now cupping her hands around her mouth to shout. "It'll be easier to get onto the treetops from here!"

I leapt down to follow her. When I landed next to Maison, we shared a grateful smile. Even though we were from different worlds and thought some of the things about the other's world were pretty weird, that was okay. Most of the time, we were on the same wavelength. We got each other, better than anyone else did.

The others jumped down, landing next to us a second later. The ledge wasn't very big, but I went as close to the building as I could, then took a giant running leap. The Endermen below me were totally unaware as I jumped over their heads and landed safely in the tree branches. For the few seconds I was in the air, it was an amazing feeling. I wondered what it would be like to fly for real, like Blue. That would make battles so much easier!

Alex and Maison jumped over next. Yancy and Destiny looked a little more uncertain, and I didn't blame them. It was a long way down.

"Here," Alex said, stringing an arrow with a lead. She shot it so that the arrow embedded itself in the side of the temple, giving Yancy and Destiny something to hold on to as they made their way across to the tree. The Endermen in the temple had reached the top story by then, and we could hear them making hostile sounds as they searched. Unlike the skeletons, the Endermen would probably follow us onto the ledge.

Destiny and Yancy exchanged a look, and then quickly grabbed the lead. Within seconds they were up in the treetops with us. Dad cut the lead to save it and then threw himself off the ledge, joining us in the tree.

We still weren't in the very top of the tree, so we used vines like ladders to climb up. Bushy jungle leaves scratched against us as we moved, but when we reached the very top, we could feel the sunlight coming straight down on us like a promise that everything was going to be okay.

"Come on!" I said, and we journeyed from treetop to treetop, Blue leading the way back to the safety of the nearby village. The haunted temple and Endermen fell back behind us.

In the end, I guessed I was glad Yancy had tamed that funny bird.

CHAPTER 24

HEN WE KNOCKED ON THE DOOR, THE VIL-
lager opened it and looked at us in shock.

"I never thought I'd see you again," he
said. "I take it you went to the temple, realized I was
right, and came back? Good thing you did. If you'd
stepped a foot into that place . . ."

"Actually," Dad said. "We went through all three
floors of the temple."

The villager's eyes widened. He stared at Dad, who
looked exhausted but okay. Then the villager stared
at me and my torn shirt. He stared at Alex, who still
looked mad that someone had dared to take away her
bow and arrows.

"I'll be," the man said. "Is what they say true? Are
there haunted ghost guards?"

"Haunted skeleton guards," Yancy said. "Probably just as bad, in their own way."

"Come in, come in," the villager said. "Let me make you something to eat. You look starved. I have some seeds for that bird as well."

"That'd be great, thanks," Yancy said. "And do you by chance have a jukebox?"

The villager looked at him strangely.

"After our night, we could use a good laugh," Yancy said. "Please and thank you."

"Sure, sure," the villager said, and started his jukebox. Like other parrots, Blue got on the ground and started happily dancing to the music. Despite all that bird had been through, he didn't look tired at all, and the dancing made him look even happier than when he was eating Oreos. I think he liked being with us. And not just because Yancy kept feeding him Earth cookies.

As we sat down and ate, recovering our strength and smiling at Blue's dancing, I said to the villager, "We want to ask you more questions about the temple. Steve Alexander was the one man who escaped from it, right? And the bad enchantments came from the Ender Dragon? Because it used to be her temple, right? Oh, oh! And who was J?"

"My son also wants to say thank you for the food," Dad said, correcting my manners.

I flushed. "Thank you," I said. Then I quickly added, "But this is really important. What do you know about . . ."

The villager was staring at me as if he couldn't believe what was coming out of my mouth. Then he said to Dad, "You have a very pushy son here."

"He's also a very good son," Dad said. "His fighting skills have improved tremendously, and he and Maison"—he gestured toward Maison—"were the ones who got the rest of us out of the dungeon."

The villager ogled me. "You escaped not just the temple, but also the dungeon itself? Are you . . . are you related to Steve Alexander?"

"I . . ." I began.

"You look a little like the statues of him." The villager sat back and thought for a minute. "They say Steve Alexander made that jungle temple."

"No, that can't be right," I said. "The Ender Dragon said it was her home. *Her* temple."

As soon as I said it, I wanted to take the words back. The villager looked at me crazily for a second, and then said, "I think you could use some sleep, son. The Ender Dragon has been trapped in the End for many, many years."

"But there was a cell for Steve Alexander," I burst out. "He couldn't have made it and imprisoned himself there!"

The jukebox stopped playing and my shout felt especially loud against the silence. Everyone stared at me, including Blue.

"I think the man is right, Stevie," Dad said. "It's time for us to all rest. We will continue investigating this mystery after we have some sleep."

"Okay, Dad," I said, but I didn't believe my thoughts were going to let me sleep any time soon.

I had thought that everything would become clearer as we found more crystal shards. Instead, it seemed to get more confusing with each adventure. I had to trust that Steve Alexander would connect all the dots in the end.

In the temple, I'd often been afraid. But we'd completed our most dangerous mission to find a crystal shard yet.

Whatever had happened in that temple thousands of years ago had changed the future of the Overworld—I was sure of it. Like Steve Alexander, I was on the path of fighting evil and bringing peace to the Overworld. Now I couldn't wait for my next mission, because it would bring me another step closer to stopping the Ender Dragon. And another step closer to finding out the truth.

READ ON FOR AN EXCITING SNEAK PEEK AT THE FOURTH BOOK IN

Danica Davidsons's
Unofficial Overworld Heroes Adventure series

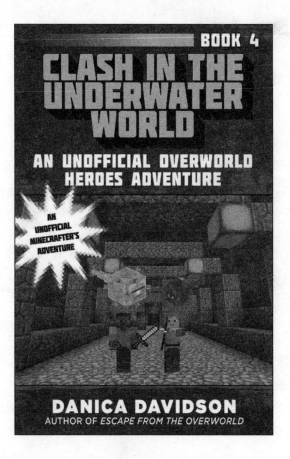

CHAPTER 1

WE WERE IN THE MIDDLE OF THE OCEAN, and we'd lost all sight of land. If anything went wrong, we were on our own.

On our little boat were Dad, my cousin Alex, my Earth friends, Maison, Destiny, and Yancy, and Yancy's newly tamed parrot, Blue. And me. But even though I was part of the Overworld Heroes task force, I felt small compared to this huge ocean with all its incredible creatures swimming just below the surface. I had had no idea how dangerous this mission would be until now—when it was too late.

Yancy wasn't helping any. In fact, he was really freaking me out.

"Hey, look at this one, Stevie," Yancy said cheerfully, showing me another picture. He'd pulled some book about ocean life on Earth out of that backpack he was always carting around. Now he was flipping through pages, showing me creatures that looked like they'd come straight from my nightmares.

I stared at the image of a hideous fish with a mouth full of row after row of fangs. On its head was a prong with a small, glowing light on the end of it, like a tiny sea lantern. If anything like that fish was waiting in the ocean below us, I'd rather just stay on the boat.

"This is an anglerfish," Yancy said. Blue, who was perched on Yancy's shoulder, whistled. "They live in the deep ocean and can grow up to three feet. They even *glow* because of bacteria down there. It's so dark in the deep ocean that you wouldn't be able to see a thing unless you bring your own light or see fish glowing. Some of the fish use their glow to lure in their prey. And the pressure is so bad down there that if you don't go in a submarine, the weight of the water will crush you."

I didn't know what being crushed by water pressure felt like, but my stomach was squeezing pretty badly on its own. And my mouth was getting dry just looking at that anglerfish.

"Yancy, stop it," Destiny sighed. "You know the ocean in *Minecraft* isn't the same as the ocean on Earth. There aren't any anglerfish here, and I don't think it gets that dark, either."

"Hey, there could be anglerfish. And who knows how dark it gets?" Yancy said. "On Earth, we're still discovering new sea life because the ocean is so big. And you know that some of the creatures we have on Earth are also in *Minecraft*. Like Blue." He gestured to his new parrot pet. Earlier, Yancy had said that being in a boat with a parrot made him look even more like a pirate. But when no one had paid much attention to that, he'd pulled out his book instead. And this agony began.

"See, look at this," Yancy said, turning another page. "A pufferfish! We have those in both places!"

Next to the anglerfish, the pufferfish looked pretty okay to me. "My dad has hunted pufferfish to make the Potion for Water Breathing," I said, looking at Dad. I wanted him to tell me that pufferfish weren't too bad. And that even though lots of the Overworld ocean hadn't been explored yet, there was no way we'd run into any anglerfish.

Unfortunately, Dad was busy looking at the map. Normally, we'd have had to go to a special cartographer in the village to get an ocean map. But we had our own special map thanks to Steve Alexander, my ancestor, who had left us the clues we needed to find Ender crystal shards that could be used to make a special weapon to defeat the Ender Dragon. Each time we completed another mission, the crystal shard we found helped us read more of Steve Alexander's magical book, which showed us where we had to go next.

Clearly, Dad wasn't going to be any help. Yancy went on, "Some people eat pufferfish on Earth, which is really dangerous if you don't do it right. They're toxic. If you eat the bad part, you'll be poisoned."

I gulped, even though I didn't have anything in my mouth. "Well, we don't like to eat pufferfish in the Overworld," I said. "Because if you do, it makes you nauseated."

"Yancy, put the book away," Maison said, her arm hanging off the side of the boat so her fingers could trail through the waves. She looked as annoyed as Destiny was with how Yancy was acting. Alex was the only one who was staring at the book with gleeful fascination. The creepier the fish, the more interested she looked.

"Not till we get to the sharks," Yancy said, flipping the pages quickly. "Here you go, Stevie. Take a look at the great white shark."

I saw an enormous mouth, even bigger than the anglerfish's, with even larger teeth. The anglerfish had lots of tiny, jutting fangs, but the great white shark had a forest of triangular teeth with jagged edges.

"The great white shark can grow up to twenty-one feet long," Yancy read.

Twenty-one feet! I never thought an anglerfish could seem safe by comparison!

"Dad," I said in a slow voice, turning to him. What I meant to say was: *Dad, please tell me Yancy is wrong and we don't have these fish here!*

"Not now, Stevie," Dad said with a frown. He was still studying the map in Steve Alexander's book. "We should be near the ocean monument holding the next crystal shard."

"Yancy, can you ride one of those?" Alex asked, pointing to the great white shark. I could tell she was already in love with the shark. "I bet they swim fast."

"If you try to ride it, it will probably eat you," Destiny said matter-of-factly.

Yancy looked up from his book in disgust. "Sharks don't go around eating people!" he said. "That's just a myth, and people believe it because they see it in movies. Sharks have more to fear from people than we do from them."

"Then what about shark attacks?" Destiny countered.

"They usually take a bite and then stop," Yancy said, as if this made everything okay. "They bite to try to figure out what something is, because they don't have hands like us. And anyway, shark attacks are incredibly rare. I'm sick of sharks getting a bad rap."

"Says the one trying to scare Stevie by showing him shark pictures," Maison muttered under her breath.

Yancy shut the book and tossed it dramatically on the floor of the boat. "I'm just trying to get us prepared for this mission. I've never been in the Overworld ocean before."

To tell the truth, I hadn't either. And that thought kept growing and growing in my head, like a puffer-fish puffing itself up.

"Hey, if you're in shark territory, you're in *their* space," Yancy went on. For some reason, he was really worked up about this. "They're just trying to eat to stay alive, and if people are being careless and in the shark's hunting grounds, they might get bitten. But don't blame the shark. It's not like in *Minecraft*, where you have hostile mobs that attack you for no clear reason."

Even though I was still nervous, I thought Yancy had an interesting point. If sharks had to eat, they had to eat, even if I thought they were scary looking. And if something unfamiliar was in the water, they had to figure out what it was, right? On the other hand, if we ran into any hostile mobs underwater—"mobs" was another word we used for "monster"—then they'd attack us just because they can, not because they need to in order to survive.

"Do you know you can pay to go under the water in a cage and have the great white sharks come right up to you?" Yancy asked. "I want to do that someday."

"Cool!" Alex cheered. "How many emeralds does it cost?"

"Why would anyone pay money for that?" Destiny asked at the same time, making a face.

"The cage keeps you safe, and there's a boat right there next to it," Yancy explained. "I heard that sharks circle their prey," Destiny said. "What if they start circling your boat?"

"I know where you're going with this, but it's not going to happen," Yancy said. "As long as you're in a boat, nothing is going to hurt you."

That's when something leapt out of the waters and landed, with a screech, in our boat.

DO YOU LIKE FICTION FOR MINECRAFTERS?

Read the Unofficial Overworld Adventure series for more of Stevie's adventures!

Escape from the
Overworld
DANICA DAVIDSON

Attack on the
Overworld
DANICA DAVIDSON

The Rise of
Herobrine
DANICA DAVIDSON

Down into the
Nether
DANICA DAVIDSON

The Armies of
Herobrine
DANICA DAVIDSON

Battle with the
Wither
DANICA DAVIDSON

Available wherever books are sold!